趣味漫畫學英語

CHINGLISH
中式英語
全破解

Agnes Chan 著

U0111410

大雨 = big rain?

新雅文化事業有限公司
www.sunya.com.hk

英語說得不中不西怎麼辦？
一書在手，踢走中式英語（Chinglish）

本書主題

全書以中式英語為主題，共有50個單元，收錄50個例子，闡釋漢語母語人士常犯的英語錯誤，全面破解中式英語！

趣味漫畫

以趣味漫畫帶出中式英語例子，對白包含錯誤示範和地道說法，形式生動，內容有趣，孩子可一邊閱讀，一邊辨別對錯。

主題分類

內容精心編排，分為兩大部分：文化差異篇 及 文法差異篇。
前者收錄因中西文化差異而出現的中式英語，包括成語、口語、中英混用表達和生活用語。
後者收錄因中英文法不同而產生的中式英語，包括單字運用、字詞搭配、句子結構。

文字解説

每個單元均有文字解說，設有 3 個欄目，剖析中英文之間的差異，並深入淺出講解英語知識，讓學童融會貫通，舉一反三。

中式英語大透視

「Hang 機」和「我的電腦 hang 了機」是常見的中英混用例子，指電腦當機了，畫面不能動。說成英文時，人們很自然直譯成 My computer is hang. 但這說法是錯誤的。在英語，正確和常用的說法是 My computer has / is frozen.、My computer is not responding / is unresponsive.

地道英文這樣說

My computer has / is frozen.

- "My computer has just frozen. Please give me a few minutes to reboot my computer," said the customer service representative. 客戶服務員說：「我的電腦剛剛當機了。請給我幾分鐘時間重新啟動電腦。」

My computer is not responding / is unresponsive.

- Tracy's computer isn't responding. I am helping her fix it. 卓思的電腦沒有反應，我正在幫她解決問題。
- My laptop is unresponsive and I can't save my document. 我的手提電腦沒有反應，無法儲存文件。

增潤詞彙加分站

電腦發生故障，當機是其中一個情況，如泛指電腦出現問題，可以說 My computer isn't working / has broken down.

- My computer isn't working. I need to upgrade its hardware. 我的電腦無法運作，我需要升級它的硬件。
- Somebody hacked into my computer last night. Now my computer has completely broken down. 昨晚有人入侵我的電腦，現在電腦完全壞掉了。

39

1 中式英語大透視

從文化及文法角度，對比中文和英文之間的差異，解釋漢語母語人士犯下英文錯誤的原因，並帶出正確的英語用字和說法。

2 地道英文這樣說

學習英語不能紙上談兵，單靠牢記知識並不足夠，因此本書收錄多條實用例句，示範如何正確使用英文詞彙、片語等。

3 增潤詞彙加分站

本欄目收錄多個英文片語、俚語、慣用語、近義詞，並提供不同範疇的英語知識，方便孩子在寫作和說話時應用出來，輕鬆搶分。

　　《中式英語全破解》是一本專門拆解中式英語（Chinglish）的語言學習圖書，旨在引導小學生辨析中式英語，避免在運用英語時受漢語思維影響。本書以有趣的方式記錄了 50 組中式英語例子，透過漫畫和解說來指出當中的錯誤，並示範正確的英語用字和說法。

　　本書劃分兩大部分，分別為文化差異篇及文法差異篇。前者探討學生因中西文化差異所犯的錯誤，後者則剖析學生因中英文法有別而犯的錯誤。文化差異篇收錄了成語、口語、中英混用表達和生活用語的例子，而文法差異篇則羅列單字運用、字詞搭配和句子結構的例子。所有內容經精心編排，例子也是精挑細選，務求讀者閱讀本書後融會貫通，把所學知識在日後應用出來。

　　書中每組例子佔一個跨頁。左頁為趣味漫畫，對白包含錯誤示範和正確說法，學童可一邊閱讀一邊辨別對錯。右頁則是文字解說，解釋小學生容易犯錯的原因，以及帶出正確的英語。另外，我們亦提供多條實用例句，示範如何正確使用英文單字、片語等。在每個單元的最後，還設增潤詞彙加分站，學童可進一步掌握單字、片語、慣用語和俚語等範疇的英語知識。

　　漢語和英語都是世界上常用的語言。透過出版本書，希望讀者能一睹這兩種美麗語言之間的有趣差異，並學習如何正確、自信地使用英語。

Agnes Chan

什麼是中式英語（Chinglish）？

中式英語（Chinglish）是漢語母語人士受其母語、文化及對世界的理解所影響而產生的英語。這類英語並不地道，讓英文母語人士聽起來不知所云。而影響我們把英語說得「不中不西」的原因主要有兩個：中西文化差異及中英文法差異。

很多中式英語是透過把中文單字、片語和慣用語直譯成英文而產生的，通常發生在雙語環境下。例如，在日常生活中，我們經常用到「食 lunch box」這組字詞和「人山人海」這個成語。說成英文時，我們很容易套入中文思維，按字面意思逐字翻譯，說成 eat lunch box 和 people mountain people sea。可是，英文母語人士缺乏漢語思維，也沒有華人的文化背景，聽到這些中式英語時，肯定無法理解當中的意思。這就是因中西文化差異而產生的中式英語。

而對英語文法規則缺乏了解，也會導致中式英語。例如，當中文母語人士不知道英文句子中詞性（parts of speech）的正確順序時，便很可能將中文的詞序應用到英語句子中，從而產生中式英語。這類由中英文法差異引起的錯誤，在本書亦可找到。

然而，我們需要留意，受世界各地文化交流影響，語言不斷演變，英文亦不例外，像 add oil（加油）這樣的中式英語已經被收錄在一些權威的詞典中。儘管如此，我們仍要明白語言需靠既定的語法規則來作為語言文字規範標準。因此，要正確使用英語，我們必須熟悉文法規則，了解文化差異，亦不忘留意英語的最新發展與變化。

文法差異篇

單字運用

字詞搭配

句子結構

你想知道嗎？

人山人海的英文是什麼？

請翻閱第 12-13 頁。

It's killing me.
是指有人要殺我嗎？

請翻閱第 30-31 頁。

為什麼飯盒不能
說成 lunch box？

請翻閱第 36-37 頁。

「我想結賬」原來不能
說成 I want to pay？

請翻閱第 62-63 頁。

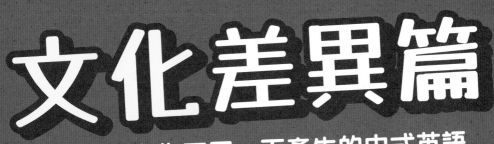

文化差異篇

因中西方文化不同，而產生的中式英語

傾盆大雨

big rain vs rain comes down in buckets

成語「傾盆大雨」指雨勢又大又急，用英文表達時，經常直譯成 **big rain**。可是，對英文母語人士來説，**big rain** 不是地道的字詞搭配，他們通常會説 heavy rain 或 downpour。另外，慣用語 rain comes down in buckets 和 rain cats and dogs 亦可用來表達相同的意思。

地道英文這樣説

heavy rain

- Traffic becomes dangerous when there is heavy rain.
  大雨時交通變得危險。

downpour

- What a downpour! Remember to take your raincoat with you.
  當真是一場傾盆大雨啊！你記得帶上雨衣。

rain comes down in buckets

- Rain was coming down in buckets right after I got off the school bus. 我下了校車後，便開始下傾盆大雨。

rain cats and dogs

- It was raining cats and dogs when we moved house yesterday. All our furniture was soaked.
  昨天我們搬家時正下着傾盆大雨，所有家具都被浸濕了。

增潤詞彙加分站

Rain 很多時帶有負面意思，代表運氣不佳。例如，慣用語 When it rains, it pours. 指當不好的事情發生，其他不如意的事情也會接踵而來，即「禍不單行」。

- I have failed my Maths test. Now, my computer is freezing. When it rains, it pours.
  我數學測驗不及格，現在電腦當機了，真是禍不單行。

28th December

Let's go to downtown on New Year's Eve.

It will be people mountain people sea. I would rather have a party at home.

What do you mean by "people mountain people sea"?

I mean it will be packed like sardines.

31st December

I was right to decide to stay home.

Are you sure? Now, there isn't enough elbow room!

成語「人山人海」指聚集的人非常多，像羣山、大海一樣，經常被逐字翻譯成 **people mountain people sea**，但英文母語人士根本無法理解這句話，因為它完全不合乎英文的語言邏輯。想正確表達「擠迫；擠擁」的意思，我們可以說 packed / squashed like sardines、not enough elbow room 等。

地道英文這樣說

packed / squashed like sardines

- People are **packed like sardines** in trains during peak hours.
  在繁忙時段，列車裏的人像沙甸魚一樣緊緊擠在一起。

not enough elbow room

- I don't like doing workouts in this small gym room. There is **not enough elbow room**.
  我不喜歡在這個小健身房運動，這裏連伸展臂肘的空間也沒有。

增潤詞彙加分站

在英語世界，我們還會用以下形容詞，來表達「擠迫；擠擁」。

crowded

- The new Korean fashion shop is very **crowded** with customers.
  新開業的韓國時裝店顧客絡繹不絕。

jammed

- The car park is **jammed** with cars. It is hard to find a way out.
  停車場泊滿了車，很難找到出路。

congested

- All roads in the areas of downtown are usually **congested** with people and cars on Christmas Eve.
  平安夜當天，市中心一帶的道路通常擠滿人和車。

小菜一碟

a small dish vs a piece of cake

Fixing the light is a small dish. It's easy!

Dad, it should be "a piece of cake".

Cooking is easy. It's a walk in the park.

Taking groceries home is easy. It's a doddle!

Getting rid of insects is easy. It's a no brainer!

在中文，我們會用「小菜一碟」比喻十分容易辦理的事。雖然把這個成語直譯為 a small dish 不是正確的英文說法，但是英文同樣會用食物來表達類似的意思——a piece of cake。另外，我們也可說 a walk in the park、a doddle、a no brainer 等。而 It's not rocket science. 也有相同含義。

地道英文這樣說

a piece of cake
- My sister is a genius. Writing essays is a piece of cake to her.
  我姊姊是天才，寫論文對她來說是小菜一碟。

a walk in the park
- Fixing home appliances is a walk in the park to Dad.
  對爸爸來說，修理家用電器真是易如反掌。

a doddle
- The Chinese test was just a doddle. I am sure I can get over 90 marks. 這次中文測驗容易至極，我肯定能考獲 90 分以上。

a no brainer
- Tony is good at playing games. Winning games is a no brainer to him. 東尼擅長玩遊戲，要在遊戲中勝出簡直輕而易舉。

It's not rocket science.
- Cooking is easy. It's not rocket science.
  烹飪很簡單，並不是火箭科學般困難。

增潤詞彙加分站

比喻事物時，我們時常用 as ... as ... 這個句式。表達「非常簡單」時，我們可以用 as easy as pie。

- Driving is as easy as pie to me. 開車對我來說不費吹灰之力。

無名小卒

a small potato vs a nobody

I'm Ivan Ho. Nice to meet you.

I'm Tony Cheung. I am new here. I'm just a small potato.

A small potato?

Ehh... I am just a nobody.

Oh, no worries.

Why are you sitting next to me?

I am just an insignificant person. We are small fry, aren't we?

成語「無名小卒」意指不重要的人。很多時我們形容自己是小人物時，會說「我只是 small potato（小薯）」。英文確實有 **small potato** 這組字詞，但它只會以眾數形式出現，而且指微不足道的事，並不是指人。「無名小卒」的地道英文是 a nobody、an insignificant / unimportant person、small fry 等。

地道英文這樣說

a nobody

• I'm just **a nobody** in this big world. I won't be able to affect the course of the world.
在這個偌大的世界，我只是無名小卒，無法影響世界的進程。

an insignificant / unimportant person

• Please don't ask me to make a decision. I am just **an insignificant person**. 請不要讓我做決定，我只是個微不足道的人。

• I am **an unimportant person** in my class. No one likes listening to me. 我在班上無足輕重，沒有人喜歡聽我說話。

small fry

• I hope the company's management team would listen to **small fry** like us. 我希望公司管理層能聽聽像我們這樣的小人物的意見。

增潤詞彙加分站

在職場上，如想表達自己地位低微，我們還可用以下慣用語。

a cog in a / the machine

• I feel frustrated that I am just **a cog in a machine**.
我感到沮喪，因為我只是機器上的一個齒輪，微不足道。

low man on the ladder

• I work as a data entry clerk. I am the **low man on the ladder**.
我是一名資料輸入員，在公司架構上我最低級。

悉隨尊便

whatever vs as you wish / like

成語「悉隨尊便」指所有事情都完全按照對方的意願去辦，不帶褒貶。用英文表達時，我們很多時會說 **Whatever**。可是，這個表達方式既沒有禮貌，意思亦有偏差，因為這等同「隨便你」，表示心中不滿，不想介入對方的做事方式。在英文，我們要留意說話時的語氣，可以有禮貌地說 as you wish / like、as you see fit、It's up to you. 等。

地道英文這樣說

as you wish / like

- "I'm not going to the job interview," said Tom.
  "You should give it a try, but well…as you wish," I replied.
  湯姆說：「我不去求職面試了。」
  我回答：「你應該嘗試一下，但是……悉隨尊便吧。」

as you see fit

- I think you look great in both shirts. Choose as you see fit.
  我覺得這兩件襯衣你都穿得很好看，選擇你喜歡的吧。

It's up to you.

- To join the trip or not, it's up to you.
  要不要參與旅行，你自己決定吧。

增潤詞彙加分站

Whatever suits you、**whatever you want** 和 **Suit yourself!** 亦可表達「隨你喜歡」，但相對上述的用語，它們比較隨便和無禮。

- All of the stationery items are in that cabinet. Take whatever you want! Here is your office desk. Suit yourself!
  所有文具都在那個櫃子裏，你想要什麼就拿什麼。這是你的辦公桌，你自便！

6 成語
一針見血
draw blood on the first prick
vs hit the bull's eye

Nowadays, children spend too much time on digital devices.

In fact, digital devices are very good tools. It depends on how they are used.

You have drawn blood on the first prick.

I have hit the bull's eye, but I haven't drawn any blood from you yet!

20

Draw blood on the first prick 是成語「一針見血」的英文直譯，可是此譯法只能讓外國人明白字面意思，即一針刺下去就見到血，而無法推測實際意思，即言論切中要害、簡明中肯。若要表達「一針見血」的真正含義，我們應用 hit the bull's eye、be spot on、hit the nail on the head 等。

地道英文這樣說

hit the bull's eye

- Miss Choi's comments about my article really hit the bull's eye. 蔡老師對我的文章的意見真是一針見血。

be spot on

- Your remarks on the football game are spot on — the Hummingbird team is the ultimate winner.
你的足球比賽評論很準確——蜂鳥隊是最終贏家。

hit the nail on the head

- Carol hit the nail on the head when she said that I am not brave enough to take on new challenges.
卡羅說我沒有勇氣接受新挑戰，她真是一語中的。

增潤詞彙加分站

Blood 跟中文「血」字的用法有很相近的地方。例如，fresh / new blood 和「新血」皆指公司新入職的員工。

- The manager brought in some fresh blood in the busiest months of the year. 經理在一年中最繁忙的月份聘請了一些新員工。

而 blood, sweat and tears 和「血汗；心血」也指人們付出的辛勞。

- The artist put in a lot of blood, sweat and tears in creating this sculpture. 藝術家創作這個雕塑時付出了很多心血。

加油

Add oil! vs Hang in there!

中文口語「加油」用作鼓勵別人加把勁，為方便表達，人們經常直譯作 **Add oil!** 這個表達極廣為使用，甚至被收錄在一些英文字典內，但是它不算是正規的英語。在英文世界，為別人打氣的說法有 **Hang in there!**、**Keep up the good work!**、**Give it your best shot!** 等。

地道英文這樣說

Hang in there!

- You are almost done with your homework. **Hang in there!**
  你的功課快完成了。堅持住！

Keep up the good work!

- "**Keep up the good work!** I am looking forward to reading your article," said Mr. Chan.
  陳老師說：「繼續努力！我很期待看你的文章。」

Give it your best shot!

- Good luck to your audition. **Give it your best shot!**
  祝你試鏡成功，把你最好的表現拿出來吧！

增潤詞彙加分站

當別人遇到挫折，我們想給予鼓勵或傳達正能量時，可用以下地道的英文語句。

Don't lose heart. 別灰心。/ **Keep your chin up.** 抬頭振作起來。

- **Don't lose heart**, Crystal! I am sure you will do better next time. **Keep your chin up!**
  小桃，不要灰心！我相信你下次會做得更好，抬頭振作起來吧！

吹水

blow water vs chat

Blow water 是廣東話俚語「吹水」的直譯，並非正確的英語。「吹水」意指朋友之間的閒談，也可以指一個人隨便説一些沒有事實根據的話，甚至是在吹牛。視乎使用的語境，英語的説法可以是 chat、chit-chat、chatter、have / make small talk。

地道英文這樣說

chat

- Sara spends hours on the phone **chatting** to her friends every day. 薩拉每天花幾個小時在電話上與朋友聊天。

chit-chat

- "What did you and Tracy talk about?" asked Billy.
  "Oh, just **chit-chat**," Kate answered.
  比利問：「你和卓思聊了什麼？」
  凱特回答：「哦，只是閒聊。」

chatter

- My younger sister likes to **chatter** about anything. She is a real chatterbox. 我妹妹喜歡什麼事情都聊一頓，她真是個話多的人。

have / make small talk

- I don't enjoy parties where I have to **make small talk** with strangers. 我不享受要與陌生人閒聊的派對。

增潤詞彙加分站

英語中的 blow sth / sb out of the water 跟廣東話俚語 blow water 看起來很相似，意思卻大不同。前者意指以壓倒性姿態戰勝或擊垮對手。

- The coach has thought of a new strategy to blow the opponents out of the water.
  教練制定了新策略來擊垮對手。

買菜

buy vegetables vs
buy groceries

Dear, can you drive me to buy vegetables for dinner today?

Sure. Are we going to eat vegetables only?

Of course not. We are going to buy vegetables, eggs, chicken wings and ribs.

So, you want to buy groceries. Let's leave home at ten.

「買菜」即廣東話的「買餸」，意指購買食材來做飯。我們很多時受中文字面意思影響，錯誤説成 **buy vegetables**。其實，我們去街市或超市，不只買蔬菜，還會買肉類和生活用品等，英文母語人士會用 groceries（食品雜貨），例如：buy / get groceries、go / do grocery shopping、go on a grocery / supermarket run。

地道英文這樣說

buy / get groceries

- Mum **buys groceries** every Monday and Thursday.
  媽媽逢星期一、四去買菜。

- There is a big sale at the supermarket. Let's **get** some **groceries** there. 超市大減價，我們去那裏買些食品雜貨吧。

go / do grocery shopping

- I will **go grocery shopping** tomorrow. Would you like to go with me? 明天我會去買菜，你想和我一起去嗎？

go on a grocery / supermarket run

- Let's **go on a supermarket run** and buy all necessary things for our end-of-year celebration.
  我們去逛逛超市，購買年末慶祝活動所需的一切東西吧。

增潤詞彙加分站

英語慣用語 run / do errands 指做跑腿或出門辦事，如：買菜、送貨、接送小孩、遛狗等。

- I need to **run a few errands** this morning, including buying groceries and walking my dog, so I can't go to the gym.
  今早我需要辦一些事，包括買雜貨和遛狗，所以我去不了健身房。

着數

jetso vs small advantages

Jetso 源自廣東話口語「着數」，指（討）便宜、（佔）好處，從別人身上獲得小益處。其實英語並沒有 **jetso** 此字，正確的説法應是 small advantages、petty gains、benefits 等。若是禮品，我們可用 freebies 或 gifts。

地道英文這樣說

small advantages

- You will get **small advantages** by becoming a member, for example, 5% off on all products.
  成為會員後，你將獲得優惠，例如所有產品可享 95 折。

petty gains

- Being obsessed with **petty gains** is a sign of greed.
  貪圖小利是貪婪的表現。

benefits

- What are the **benefits** of buying the care plan for my mobile phone? 購買手機保用計劃有什麼好處？

freebies / gifts

- "Will I get some **freebies** after joining the club?" asked James. "You will get two **gifts** — a shopping bag and a tube of massage cream," answered the shop assistant.
  詹姆斯問：「加入俱樂部後我會得到贈品嗎？」
  店員回答：「你會得到兩件禮品 —— 一個購物袋和一枝按摩膏。」

增潤詞彙加分站

Advantage 還可解作「利用」，請看 take advantage of 這個片語。

- Kimmy **took advantage of** David's kindness and asked him to buy her jewellery.
  嘉莉利用大衛的好意，要求他買珠寶送給她。

笑死我了

Laugh die me! vs It's killing me!

Laugh die me! 是廣東話口語「笑死我了」的直譯，不是正確的英語。「笑死我了」是非常誇張的説法，意指事情令人發笑得快要死掉。其實英文也有類似表達，如：laugh (somebody's) head off，字面意思是「笑到頭斷掉」。另可視乎語境，使用 It's / You're killing me!、It's hilarious!、crack (somebody) up 等。

地道英文這樣説

laugh (somebody's) head off

- My brother laughed his head off when he saw me fall from the chair. 哥哥看到我從椅子上摔下來時，笑得前仰後合。

It's / You're killing me!

- Look at this comic strip. It's so funny. It's killing me! 看看這篇漫畫，太有趣了，笑死我了！

It's hilarious!

- The latest Mr. Bean movie is full of funny scenes. It's hilarious! 最新的《憨豆先生》電影有很多有趣的場景，十分滑稽！

crack (somebody) up

- The new TV programme is extremely funny. Every episode cracks me up. 新的電視節目十分有趣，每一集都讓我笑瘋。

增潤詞彙加分站

英語慣用語 Don't make me laugh. 並不是指別讓我笑，而是指當聽到荒謬或不可信的事情時，示意説話一方別開玩笑了。

- You bought me a new smart phone? Don't make me laugh. You are not that generous.
  你買了一部新的智能電話給我？別跟我開玩笑了，你可沒那麼慷慨。

面青青

look green vs look pale

Jesse, how are you?

Are you okay? You look green.

Do I have green paints on my face?

No. I mean you look pale.

I didn't have any breakfast this morning.

You can have my sandwich.

Thank you, Grace.

廣東話口語「面青青」指因身體不舒服或受驚嚇而臉色變青，時常被直譯成 look green，但這不是地道的英語説法。英語中，我們可用 look pale、look as white as a sheet / ghost、look green around the gills 等。

地道英文這樣說

look pale

- You **look pale**. Let's sit down and take a rest.
  你看起來臉色蒼白，坐下來休息一下吧。

look as white as a sheet / ghost

- You **look as white as a sheet**. Have you eaten anything this morning? 你的臉看起來像紙一樣白，今早你有吃東西嗎？

- Lucy **looked as pale as a ghost** after her ride on the roller coaster. 露西坐完過山車後，臉色蒼白如鬼。

look green around the gills

- Kate **looks green around the gills**. She has already vomited twice this morning. 凱特臉色蒼白，她今早已經吐了兩次。

增潤詞彙加分站

形容詞 petrified 及慣用語 scare the life out of (somebody) 亦可用來表達相同意思。

petrified

- My brother was **petrified** as a black bear approached him.
  當黑熊接近弟弟時，他嚇呆了。

scare the life out of (somebody)

- The appearance of a lady in a long white dress on the road after midnight **scared the life out of the taxi driver**.
  午夜後路上出現一位身穿白色長裙的女士，嚇得的士司機魂飛魄散。

There will be no school this Friday!

Really? Let's double confirm it with the school calendar.

Do you mean I should reconfirm it?

Yes.

Mum, you're right. It's a school day this Friday.

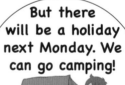

But there will be a holiday next Monday. We can go camping!

把「請再確認一下」説成「請 double confirm 一下」，是中式英語的經典例子。雖然 double 有「雙重；兩倍」的意思，但是 reconfirm 才是「再確認」的正確用詞。re 帶「再次；重新」之意，有時可和 double 通用，有時則不能。若我們對事情感疑惑，想再檢查、確認一次，亦可用 double-check、make sure。

地道英文這樣說

reconfirm

- Can you reconfirm your last name with me?
  你能再次與我確認你的姓氏嗎？

- I have just reconfirmed your booking with Dr. Ng on 4th December. 我剛剛再次確認了你與吳醫生在 12 月 4 日的預約。

double-check

- Please double-check your account number. There is a missing number. 請再檢查一下你的賬號，它缺少了一個數字。

make sure

- Please make sure that you have written down your name on the exam paper. 請確保在試卷上寫上你的名字。

增潤詞彙加分站

另外一個與 reconfirm 意思差不多的字詞是 verify，意指「驗證」，用於較嚴謹或正式的情況，以充分證據確認事情或真相。

- I am sending you a link via email. Please click on it to verify your email address.
  我將透過電郵向你發送連結，請點擊它來驗證你的電郵地址。

- The police has verified that two burglars have been caught.
  警方證實兩名賊人已被抓獲。

吃午餐盒

eat lunch box vs
eat boxed lunch

What are you eating?

I am eating my lunch box.

Is your lunch box edible?

I mean I am eating my boxed lunch. Would you like some fried rice?

No, thanks. I have got my packed meal.

人們説「吃午餐盒」時，經常會中英混用，説成「吃 lunch box」。但是，**box** 是盒子，不能吃進肚子，正確的説法應是 boxed / box lunch、packed lunch / meal。若自備的午餐是用袋子裝的，如：三文治、水果，則可用 bagged / bag lunch 或 bagged / bag meal，用 packed lunch / meal 亦可。

地道英文這樣説

boxed / box lunch

• There is no canteen at the museum, so we should bring our **boxed lunch**.
博物館內沒有食堂，所以我們要自備午餐。

packed lunch / meal

• I bring my **packed lunch** to school every day.
我每天都會自攜午餐到學校。

bagged / bag lunch; bagged / bag meal

• It takes ten minutes for me to prepare my **bagged lunch**.
我需要十分鐘時間來準備袋裝午餐。

增潤詞彙加分站

雖然 boxed / box lunch、packed lunch / meal、bagged / bag lunch 在字面上沒有指明午餐是在家中預備，但在大部分情況下，此含意是不言而喻的。若想明確表明食物在家中預備，可用 **home-packed meal** 來表達。

• Your **home-packed meal** looks so delicious. There are appetisers, a main dish and a dessert.
你家中預備的餐點看起來很美味，有前菜、主菜和甜點。

電腦當機

My computer is hang. vs My computer is frozen.

Dad, my computer is hang. I cannot save my document.

Are you hanging your computer in the air?

No. It's not hanging in the air. It is frozen.

You can simply reboot your computer.

「Hang 機」和「我的電腦 hang 了機」是常見的中英混用例子，指電腦當機了，畫面不能動。説成英文時，人們很自然直譯成 **My computer is hang.** 但這説法是錯誤的。在英語，正確和常用的説法是 My computer has / is frozen.、My computer is not responding / is unresponsive.

地道英文這樣說

My computer has / is frozen.

- **"My computer has** just **frozen.** Please give me a few minutes to reboot my computer," said the customer service representative. 客戶服務員説：「我的電腦剛剛當機了。請給我幾分鐘時間重新啟動電腦。」

My computer is not responding / is unresponsive.

- **Tracy's computer isn't responding.** I am helping her fix it. 卓思的電腦沒有反應，我正在幫她解決問題。

- **My laptop is unresponsive** and I can't save my document. 我的手提電腦沒有反應，無法儲存文件。

增潤詞彙加分站

電腦發生故障，當機是其中一個情況，如泛指電腦出現問題，可以説 My computer isn't working / has broken down.

- **My computer isn't working.** I need to upgrade its hardware. 我的電腦無法運作，我需要升級它的硬件。

- Somebody hacked into my computer last night. Now **my computer has** completely **broken down.** 昨晚有人入侵我的電腦，現在電腦完全壞掉了。

售貨員

sales vs salesperson

I bought the suit last week. Can I talk to the sales who helped me.

Do you mean you want to find out our volume of sales?

Nope.

Oh! You want to talk to the salesperson. He will be with you shortly.

Hi, Mr. Chan. I am Keith, the salesman who served you. What can I do for you?

The sleeves are too short. Look!

廣東話「sale 屎」指售貨員、推銷員，由英文字 **sales** 演變出來，常夾雜在中文口語表達中。但 **sales** 的真正意思是銷售量，而非賣東西的人。我們可按實際情況用 salesperson / salesman / saleswoman、shop assistant / sales clerk、sales representative / rep 等，意思如下。

地道英文這樣說

salesperson 售貨員 / **salesman** 男售貨員 / **saleswoman** 女售貨員

- All **salespersons** should be able to explain their product features. 所有售貨員都應該能夠解釋產品的特點。

shop assistant / **sales clerk** 店員

- I enjoy being a **shop assistant** as I like meeting people from all walks of life. 我喜歡當店員，因為我喜歡認識各行各業的人。

- Let's ask the **sales clerk** to find the right size for you. 我們去請店員為你尋找合適的尺寸吧。

sales representative / **rep** 銷售代表

- The **sales representative** selected a very good Internet package for me. 那銷售代表為我選擇了一個非常好的網絡服務組合。

- The **sales rep** was so rude to me. I am going to file a complaint. 那銷售代表對我非常無禮，我要投訴。

增潤詞彙加分站

一些銷售代表除了銷售產品外，還提供客戶服務，我們通常稱呼他們為 **customer service representative**。

- The **customer service representative** on the phone taught me patiently how to pay my fees via the Internet. 電話裏的客戶服務代表耐心地教我如何在網上繳交費用。

Excuse me. Where can I find some tissue paper?

Here you go.

No. I am looking for tissues in a box.

Oh, I see. You are looking for boxed tissues.

Thank you for your help.

在中文,「紙巾」泛指廁紙、盒裝紙巾、廚房紙、餐巾紙等紙造產品,我們時常中英混用,以 tissue (paper) 統稱它們,例如説「我想要一張 tissue (paper)」。在英語,表達不同種類的紙巾時,需用不同名詞,如:廁紙是 toilet paper;盒裝紙巾是 boxed / box / facial tissue;廚房紙是 paper towel;餐巾紙則是 napkin。

地道英文這樣說

toilet paper

• Mum, why can't I find any toilet paper in the washroom?
媽媽,為什麼我在洗手間找不到廁紙?

boxed / box / facial tissue

• Karen wiped her face with a piece of facial tissue.
凱倫用了一張面紙擦臉。

paper towel

• Mum likes using paper towels to soak excessive water from raw meat. 媽媽喜歡用廚房紙吸去生肉中多餘的水分。

napkin

• Judith bought us some napkins. Let's put them on the plates.
茱蒂買了一些的餐巾紙給我們,我們把它們放在碟子上吧。

增潤詞彙加分站

Tissue paper 一詞,對於英文母語人來説,是放進禮盒內,用來保護禮品的內襯紙(俗稱「雪梨紙」),即 gift wrapping tissue paper。至於用來包裹禮盒的包裝紙(俗稱「花紙」),則是 wrapping paper,不用加 tissue 這字。

有男子氣概的　man vs manly

「好 man」這個中英混用表達,形容某人很有男子氣概。但是,英文字 man 是名詞,指「成年男子」,不能用作形容人物。在英語,「具男子氣概」應說成 manly、masculine 等。前者帶有強壯的意思,近義詞有 robust、sturdy。

地道英文這樣說

manly

- Those trainers at the gym are so manly. All of them are very strong. 健身房裏的那些教練很有男子氣概,他們都十分強壯。

masculine

- Masculine men are strong and powerful.
  有男子氣概的男人強而有力。

robust

- My brother has become very robust since he started exercising.
  自從哥哥開始運動後,變得非常強壯。

sturdy

- John has a sturdy body. He could finish a marathon in three hours. 約翰擁有強健體魄,他可以在三小時內跑完馬拉松。

增潤詞彙加分站

形容男士有男子氣概、健壯迷人,可用俚語 a hunk of a man。

- Andy is a hunk of a man. He is so strong and muscular.
  安迪健壯迷人,他是如此的強壯和肌肉發達。

另外,我們也可用慣用語 as strong as an ox 來形容強壯的人。

- Patrick is as strong as an ox. He can carry all of the heavy boxes in one go. 派崔克強壯如牛,他可一口氣搬動所有重箱子。

黑眼圈

black eyes vs dark circles

Good morning! You look so tired with your black eyes.

Mine are called dark circles. I stayed up late to finish my essay.

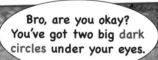

Bro, are you okay? You've got two big dark circles under your eyes.

Mine are called black eyes. I got hit in the eyes last night.

「黑眼圈」是指因睡眠不足而令眼睛周圍的皮膚變暗,常被直譯為 **black eyes**。再加上「黑眼圈」俗稱「熊貓眼」,更令這個譯法變得順理成章,但其實 **black eyes** 指眼睛因被打或撞傷後所產生的瘀青。「黑眼圈」的正確說法應是 dark circles、dark circles under eyes 或 dark under-eye circles。

dark circles

- How can I get rid of my dark circles? 如何去除黑眼圈?

dark circles under eyes

- I go to bed early to avoid having dark circles under my eyes the next morning. 為了避免翌日早上出現黑眼圈,我習慣早睡。

dark under-eye circles

- This cream helps lighten your dark under-eye circles. 這款眼霜有助減淡黑眼圈。

除了黑眼圈,另一種常見的生理狀況是眼袋。眼袋可稱為 bag under eyes 或 under-eye bags,或可形容為 puffy eyes。

bag under eyes / under-eye bags

- Are there any treatments for under-eye bags? 有沒有治療眼袋的方法?

puffy eyes

- I usually have puffy eyes if I drink lots of water before bedtime the night before.
如果前一晚睡前喝很多水,翌日早上我通常會眼袋浮腫。

嘴巴大

big mouth vs wide mouth

Do you know who the girl with a pong tail is?

I've heard that her family is rich. Her parents earn a lot.

The girl has a big mouth. She would look beautiful if she had a smaller mouth.

She doesn't have a big mouth. You do! My daughter looks beautiful with her wide mouth.

中式英語大透視

描述物件外形大時，我們慣常用 **big**，例如用 **big mouth** 形容嘴巴大。**Big mouth** 在文法上是正確的，但另有意思，指某人多嘴多舌，說出不該說或本應保密的話；而嘴巴外形大的正確說法是 wide mouth。我們要多留意英文形容詞的實際意思，謹慎選詞用字。

地道英文這樣說

big mouth

- Amy has such a big mouth that she has told our whole class about your secrets.
  艾米有一張大嘴巴，她已經把你的秘密告訴我們全班了。

wide mouth

- A woman with a wide mouth can be beautiful too.
  嘴巴大的女人也可以很漂亮。

增潤詞彙加分站

英文還有很多字詞可用來形容嘴巴，例如：

dainty mouth 櫻桃小嘴

- The little girl with a dainty mouth is adorable.
  那個擁有櫻桃小嘴的小女孩可愛極了。

full-lipped mouth 厚唇的嘴巴

- Uncle Tom is a strong man with a full-lipped mouth.
  湯姆叔叔是個嘴唇豐厚的強壯男人。

thin-lipped mouth 薄唇的嘴巴

- The boy with a thin-lipped mouth is my youngest brother.
  那個薄唇男孩是我最小的弟弟。

當你懊悔自己保守不住秘密時，可以說 Me and my big mouth!

- I shouldn't have told you all these. Me and my big mouth!
  我不該告訴你這些，都怪我的大嘴巴！

wash my head vs wash my hair

Oh no. I need to wash my head.

You need to wash your hair instead.

Not again!

I guess you really need to wash your head now.

把「洗頭」譯成英文時，我們會受中文思維影響，說成 **wash my head**。但我們知道，所謂「洗頭」其實是指洗頭髮、頭皮。在英語世界，正確用字是 wash / shampoo my hair。

洗頭時，我們常使用護髮素護理頭髮，英文是 apply conditioner 或 condition my hair。其他描述洗頭過程的動詞還有 lather（用手打出泡沫）、leave ... on（讓……留在）、rinse（沖洗）。

地道英文這樣說

wash my hair / shampoo my hair

- Mum **washes her hair** every day with her favourite perfumed shampoo. 媽媽每天都用她最喜歡的香氛洗髮水洗頭。

apply conditioner / condition my hair

- I always **apply conditioner** after shampooing my hair. 我用洗髮水洗頭後，都會使用護髮素。

lather

- I **lather** a coin-sized amount of shampoo and apply it to my scalp. 我用手將硬幣大小的洗髮水打出泡沫，然後塗抹在頭皮上。

leave ... on; rinse

- **Leave** the conditioner **on** your hair for a few minutes. Then **rinse** it out thoroughly with warm water. 將護髮素留在頭髮上幾分鐘，然後用暖水徹底沖洗。

增潤詞彙加分站

諺語 **wash (somebody) out of my hair** 意指跟某人結束關係，如情侶分手，並抹去與此人有關的記憶。

- Susan has **washed Jayden out of her hair** as if he had never existed. 蘇珊已經把傑登忘掉了，就好像他從來沒有存在過。

前天

yesterday's yesterday vs two days ago

We first met each other yesterday's yesterday.

Eh... yesterday's yesterday?

I am so sad that you forgot when we first met.

We first met on Valentine's Day. Don't you remember?

You mean we first met two days ago. Please wait!

「昨天」的英文是 **yesterday**，但是「昨天的昨天（前天）」的英文並不是 yesterday's yesterday。正確的說法是 two days ago 或 the day before yesterday。在英文口語中，我們亦可用 two days back 或 two days earlier 來表達「兩天前」。

地道英文這樣說

two days ago

- Larry has been ill since two days ago.
  拉里自兩天前就生病了。

the day before yesterday

- Mum bought me a guitar the day before yesterday.
  媽媽前天買了一把結他給我。

two days back

- I left my mobile phone on a taxi two days back.
  兩天前我把手機遺留在的士上了。

two days earlier

- You borrowed my pen two days earlier. Can I have it back?
  兩天前你借了我的筆，我可以拿回它嗎？

增潤詞彙加分站

在英文世界，有一些有趣的諺語與「昨天」有關，如 not be born yesterday、yesterday's news。

not be born yesterday 不是昨天出生（指不是那麼愚蠢）

- I don't believe what you've just said. I wasn't born yesterday.
  我不相信你剛才說的話，我可不是那麼愚蠢。

yesterday's news 過時的事物（指該事物不再有趣）

- The old toys in the cabinet are yesterday's news to Jason.
  櫃子裏的舊玩具對傑森來說不再有趣了。

Two weeks later 是中文「兩星期後」的直譯，但它通常用於已過去的事情。如要說事情會在兩星期後發生，我們應該用 in two weeks' time 或 in two weeks。

另外，亦有人會誤用 within two weeks 來表達「兩星期後」，但它指事情會於兩星期內任何時間發生或完成，不會超過兩星期。

地道英文這樣說

in two weeks' time

- My piano exam is coming up in two weeks' time. I'm feeling nervous. 兩周後便是鋼琴考試，我很緊張。

in two weeks

- My brother is returning home from the UK in two weeks. 兩周後哥哥將從英國回家。

two weeks later

- We went to Taipei last month. Two weeks later, we drove to Kaohsiung. 上月我們去了台北，兩星期後，我們駕車前往高雄。

within two weeks

- Don't worry. I will finish my part within two weeks. 別擔心，我會在兩周內完成我負責的部分。

增潤詞彙加分站

Fortnight 解作「十四天」，即兩星期。我們可用 in a fortnight 來表達「兩星期後」。Fortnight 屬舊式英語，在美國和加拿大已甚少使用，但英國或被英國文化影響較深的地方仍有使用。

- Your appointment is in a fortnight. Please come at 4 p.m. 你的預約是在兩星期後，請於下午四時前來。

兩周後的周五

next next Friday vs the Friday after next (week)

Your next appointment is next next Friday at 2 pm.

Today is a Wednesday, so your next appointment is the Friday after next week.

And remember to take an X-ray next next Thursday.

Do you mean the Thursday after next week?

中文「下星期」可譯作 **next week**，而「下星期五」則是 **next Friday**。那麼「下下星期（下星期再下星期）」的英文可順理成章直譯為 **next next week** 嗎？「下下星期五（下個再下個星期五）」又是什麼？前者的英文應是 the week after next (week)，而後者則應是 the Friday after next (week) 或 the Friday of the week after next week 等。

地道英文這樣說

next week

* Sarah will fly to the US for a meeting next week.
  莎拉下周將飛往美國參加會議。

next Friday

* There will be no school next Friday. 下周五不用上課。

the week after next (week)

* I am preparing hard for my exam that will take place in the week after next (week).
  我正在努力準備下下星期（下星期再下星期）的考試。

the Friday after next (week) /
the Friday of the week after next week

* Grandma's 98th birthday is on the Friday after next (week).
  下下星期五（下個再下個星期五）是祖母的 98 歲生日。

增潤詞彙加分站

英語有一些俚語與「星期五」有關，如 Thank God it's Friday! 意思是「謝天謝地，今天是星期五」，為一周工作結束而高興。

* Thank God it's Friday! Let's go for a drink!
  謝天謝地，今天是星期五！我們去喝一杯吧！

給你的

Give you. vs Here you go.

Give you... give you... your wallet!

Oh... Thank you so much!

Here you go, a little toy car! You deserve to have a treat!

把東西遞給別人或送禮給別人時，我們會説「（這是）給你的」。換成英文時，就很自然譯作 **Give you.** 可是，這個説法並不正確，地道的説法應是 Here you go!、There you go!、Here it is!、Here they are! 若對方是長輩，説 Here you are!、There you are! 會比較有禮貌。

地道英文這樣説

Here you go! / There you go! / Here it is!

- Thanks for letting me borrow your suitcase. I'm returning it to you. Here you go! 謝謝你把行李箱借給我，現在還給你！

Here they are!（用於眾數）

- "I've baked some cookies. Here they are!" said Aunt Daisy. 黛西姨姨説：「我烤了一些曲奇餅，給你們的！」

Here you are! / There you are!

- "I've finished my report. Here you are, Mr. White," said Chris. 里斯説：「我完成報告了。懷特老師，這是交予你的。」

增潤詞彙加分站

若把某物給予別人時，想加強驚喜效果，我們可説 Voilà! 或 Ta-da! 前者源自法文，意指 **there**。

Voilà!

- I spent two days decorating the living room for our Christmas party. Voilà! 我為了聖誕派對花了兩天來裝飾客廳。瞧！

Ta-da!

- Mum, just close your eyes and walk forward. Ta-da! Here's our birthday present to you! 媽媽，閉上眼睛，往前走。嗒噠！這是我們送給你的生日禮物！

Do it slowly. vs Take your time.

當我們叫別人「慢慢來」時，很自然誤譯為 Do it slowly. 兩者的字面意思相近，但是實際意思有點不同。「慢慢來」是鼓勵別人不用急，用適合自己的速度去完成事情，而 Do it slowly. 是叫人慢慢地做事。「慢慢來」真正的英文説法應是 Take your time. 我們亦可説 There's no need to rush.、at your own pace 等。

地道英文這樣說

Take your time.

- You can read all the guidelines before working. Take your time. 你可以在工作前先閱讀所有守則。慢慢來，不用急。

There is no need to rush.

- The bus won't arrive in an hour. There is no need to rush. 巴士一小時後才到達，無需着急。

at your own pace

- You can work on the essay at your own pace. There's no time restriction. 你可以按照自己的速度寫論文，沒有時間限制。

增潤詞彙加分站

我們亦可使用以下諺語，分別説明時間充裕或時間太多。

Time is on (somebody's) side.

- We don't have to hand in our report until next month, so time is on our side. 我們到下月才需呈交報告，時間很充裕。

too much time on (somebody's) hands

- My brother has just quit his job. He has too much time on his hands. 哥哥剛辭職，他現在有太多的時間了。

我想結賬

I want to pay. vs Can I have the bill, please?

Son, can you ask for the bill, please?

Sure.

I want to pay!

You should politely say to the waitress "Can I have the bill, please?"

Can I have the bill, please?

Of course.

在餐廳用餐後想付款時，我們會說「我想付款」。在英語，我們卻很少說 I want to pay. 因為這太直接和不禮貌了。英語母語人士通常較委婉，會以問題形式表達所想，例如：Can I have the bill / check, please?、Could we get the bill / check, please?、Would you please bring me the bill / check?，亦可說 Check, please!

Can I have the bill / check, please?

• Excuse me, **can I have the bill, please?** I would like to pay by cash. 打擾一下，請問可以給我賬單嗎？我想用現金支付。

Could we get the bill / check, please?

• It's about time for us to go. **Could we get the bill, please?** 我們該走了，請問可以給我賬單嗎？

Would you please bring me the bill / check?

• **Would you please bring me the check?** Do you accept credit card payments? 請將賬單拿給我好嗎？你們接受信用卡付款嗎？

Check, please!

• **"Check, please!"** Kate said to the busy waitress. 凱特對那個忙碌的女侍應說：「請給我賬單，謝謝！」

在外國，分攤飯餐費用是很常見的。付款或下單前，對侍應說 **Please put this on separate bills / checks for us.** 便可。

• We're splitting our bill, so **please put this on separate bills for us.** 我們分開付款，所以請分開我們的賬單。

我來請客

I pay. vs It's on me.

中國人喜歡請客，結賬時常説「我來請客」。款待外國人時，很自然會説 I pay. 但這不合乎英文文法，要説成 I'll pay for the meal. 才正確。不過，英文母語人士較常用的語句其實是 It's on me!、Let me get this.、It's my treat! / My treat!

地道英文這樣說

I'll pay for the meal.

- Order whatever you like to eat. I'll pay for the meal.
  想吃什麼就點什麼，我來付錢。

It's on me!

- "It's your birthday today, so it's on me!" Janice said to me.
  賈妮絲對我說：「今天是你的生日，由我來請客吧。」

Let me get this.

- I have just received my bonus. Let me get this.
  我剛剛收到花紅，讓我來請客吧。

It's my treat! / My treat!

- "Let's go to have a drink after work. It's my treat!" the manager said. 經理說：「下班後我們去喝一杯。我請客！」

增潤詞彙加分站

一些餐廳可能贈送前菜或飲品，我們可用 on the house 來表達。可世上沒有免費午餐 (free lunch)，我們還是腳踏實地較好。

on the house

- All drinks were on the house at Lala Moon Restaurant last weekend. 上周末，蘭木餐廳的所有飲料都是免費的。

There's no such thing as a free lunch.

- There's no such thing as a free lunch. You've got to work hard. 世上沒有免費午餐，你必須努力工作。

當別人向你道謝時，我們常回應「不用客氣」。在英語世界，這種回應也很常見，但不能直譯成 No need to thank me. 想地道自然地表達相同意思，我們可以説 No problem (at all).、No worries. / Don't worry about it.、It was / It's nothing.

地道英文這樣說

No problem (at all).

- "Thanks for your help," said Jesse.
  "No problem. I'm glad to help," replied Cherry.
  傑西說：「謝謝你的幫助。」
  小櫻回答：「小意思，我很高興能幫上忙。」

No worries. / Don't worry about it.

- "Thanks for helping me with the Maths problems," said Kelly.
  "Don't worry about it. Anytime," replied Jay.
  凱利說：「謝謝你解答我的數學問題。」
  英傑回答：「不用客氣，我隨時也可幫忙。」

It was / It's nothing.

- "Thanks for opening the door for me," said Jane.
  "It was nothing," said Hayden.
  簡愛說：「謝謝你為我開門。」
  海登說：「很小事，不用謝。」

增潤詞彙加分站

在較正式的場合，則可使用 Don't mention it.、My pleasure.、You're welcome.

- "Thanks for completing the survey for me," said Fion.
  "You're welcome," said Mr. Chan.
  菲安說：「感謝你為我完成問卷調查。」
  陳先生說：「不用客氣。」

不用找續

Keep the money. vs Keep the change.

付款時，有時我們不想要太多零錢，便叫收銀員不用找續。人們很多時誤譯作 Keep the money. 原因是他們用 money 泛指所有錢，或不清楚零錢的英文是 change。要表達「不用找續」，英文母語人士慣用以下語句：Keep the change.、Keep / Save the rest.、Just keep it.、No change is needed.

地道英文這樣說

Keep the change.

- "Here's 20 dollars. Just keep the change," Mrs Chan said to the shop clerk. 陳太對店員說：「這裏有 20 元，不用找續。」

Keep / Save the rest.

- I only have a 100-dollar booknote with me. This meal costs 85 dollars. Just keep the rest as tips.
  我身上只有一張 100 元的鈔票，這頓飯 85 元，剩下的就當作小費吧。

Just keep it.

- "Here's your change," the shop assistant said.
  "Oh. Just keep it," said John.
  店員說：「這是要找續的零錢。」
  約翰說：「哦，不用找續了。」

No change is needed.

- No change is needed. I don't like keeping coins.
  不用找續，我不喜歡收硬幣。

增潤詞彙加分站

Change 除了指找續用的零錢，亦指換開的零錢，即用硬幣及較小單位的貨幣換取相同金額的紙幣和較大的貨幣。

- Can you give me 50 dollars in change?
  你能給我 50 元的零錢嗎？

你想知道嗎？

「廚師」的英文不是 cooker 嗎？

請翻閱第 72-73 頁。

hear 和 listen to 有什麼分別？

請翻閱第 90-91 頁。

No, I am OK. 這句句子錯在哪裏？

請翻閱第 102-103 頁。

文法差異篇

因中英語文法不同，而產生的中式英語

單字運用

廚師

cooker vs cook

What does your father do?

He is a cooker.

Your dad can't be a cooker. I guess you meant to say he is a cook, right?

Oh, yes! His boss said he is a wonderful cook.

在中文，很多職業以「師」結尾，例如：老師、律師、設計師、攝影師。而英語也有類似情況，不少職業以 **er** 作結，例如：**teacher**、**lawyer**、**designer**、**photographer**。這使我們以偏概全，誤以為「師」和 **er** 對應，把「廚師」說成 cooker。其實，cooker 指「爐具；廚灶」，而「廚師」的英文可以是 cook，拼寫和動詞 cook 一樣，泛指「做飯的人」。

地道英文這樣說

cooker

- Our **cooker** isn't working, so we have ordered takeaway.
  我們的煮食爐壞了，所以我們叫了外賣。

- A pressure **cooker** can be used as a yogurt maker and a slow **cooker**. 壓力鍋可用作乳酪機和慢燉鍋。

cook

- My mum is a great **cook**. She prepares delicious dishes for us.
  媽媽廚藝出色，她為我們準備美味的菜餚。

- Uncle Gavin works as a **cook** in a nearby restaurant.
  加文叔叔在附近的餐廳當廚師。

增潤詞彙加分站

除了 cook 以外，chef 也解作「廚師」，但通常指「（餐廳或酒店的）大廚；主廚」。

- The **chef** is instructing his kitchen staff how to prepare dishes for the wedding banquet.
  主廚正在指導廚房員工如何準備婚宴菜餚。

- A successful **chef** must be equipped with outstanding cooking skills, creativity and leadership.
  成功的主廚必須具備出色的烹飪技巧、創意和領導能力。

寶寶　baby vs toddler

Hayden, Hayden, where are you?

My son is missing! He's just a baby.

Was he in a stroller?

Mum!

He's not a baby. He's a toddler.

在中文口語，我們會用「寶寶 (baby)」泛指初生嬰兒至幾歲的幼童，但其實「寶寶」可以分為「嬰兒」、「學步幼童」和「兒童」。在英語，這種區分比較鮮明，我們通常會用 baby 指未能步行及說話的嬰幼兒；toddler 指一至三歲小孩；preschooler 指四至五歲兒童。若再細分，「嬰兒」更可分為新生嬰兒，即 newborn (baby)。

地道英文這樣說

baby

• Look! The baby in the stroller is so adorable.
看！嬰兒車裏的嬰兒真是太可愛了。

toddler

• The toddler tumbled down to the floor and started crying.
那個幼童跌倒在地，開始哭泣。

preschooler

• Several preschoolers are playing games in the park.
幾個學齡前兒童正在公園裏玩遊戲。

newborn (baby)

• The newborn next door was crying loudly last night. I could hardly sleep. 昨晚隔壁的初生嬰兒哭得很大聲，我幾乎無法入睡。

增潤詞彙加分站

有一些英文俚語和諺語與「寶寶」有關，例如：

bundle of joy 新生嬰兒

• Uncle Peter and Aunt Lisa have brought their bundle of joy home. 彼得叔叔和麗莎姨姨把他們剛出生的小寶寶帶回家了。

打架

argument vs fight

Are you OK? You look sad.

I had a fight with my brother yesterday.

Oh no. Did you get hurt?

Why would I get hurt?

Didn't you fight and hit each other?

A fight means an argument, not necessarily involving physical forces.

So, what was the fight about?

It was a quarrel about which TV program to watch.

表達雙方發生肢體或言語衝突時，中文有很多詞語可選擇，如：打架、打鬥、吵架、爭拗；英文也同樣，如：fight、argument、quarrel。需留意的是，fight 除了解作「打架」，亦可指「吵架；爭拗」；至於 argument 和 quarrel，則只解作言語上的衝突，我們切忌混淆。

地道英文這樣說

fight

- I have just had a fight with my sister. I am not going to talk to her today. 我剛剛和姊姊吵架，我今天不會和她說話。

argument

- Crystal and I had an argument over what birthday gift to buy for Elisa. 我和小晶為買什麼生日禮物給艾莎而爭吵了。

quarrel

- Stop the quarrel over what food to eat for lunch. You eat what I cook for you. 不要爭論午餐吃什麼了。我煮什麼，你就吃什麼。

增潤詞彙加分站

Dispute 亦可解作「爭拗」，但主要用於僱主及僱員、國與國之間，並且多指需要律師等人員介入處理的紛爭。

- The airline and its workers still haven't resolved their dispute over the leave arrangement.
  航空公司與員工就休假安排的爭議仍未解決。

英文有一些關於「不再爭拗；忘記恩怨」的慣用語，例如：

bury the hatchet 冰釋前嫌

- Doris and Zoe decided to bury the hatchet and be friends again. 朵麗絲和佐伊決定冰釋前嫌，做回朋友。

去（某地）

come vs go

Let's go to the theatre.

Movie tickets are too expensive. How about coming to your place?

Do you mean going to my place?

Yes. We can watch a movie on the Internet.

SUPERMARKET

Good idea. Let's go to the supermarket to buy some snacks.

Come 和 go 這兩個動詞常被混淆。Come 指「來；過來」，所表示的方向是朝向說話者的位置，如：**come to school**（來上學）、**come here**（來這兒）。Go 指「去；過去」，所表示的方向是離開說話者的位置，如：**go to school**（去上學）、**go there**（去那兒）。

地道英文這樣說

come

- "When will you **come** home today?" Mum asked me.
  媽媽問我：「你今天什麼時候回家？」

- Colin, **come** and sit with me.
  柯林，過來和我一起坐。

go

- How does your dad **go** to work every day?
  你爸爸每天怎麼去上班？

- Danny **goes** swimming every Friday evening.
  丹尼每周五晚上去游泳。

增潤詞彙加分站

Come 和 go 是很常用的英文字，在很多諺語及片語也被使用。

come and go 來來去去；時有時無

- It is very strange that the rash **comes and goes**.
  這皮疹時有時無，很奇怪。

on the go 很忙碌

- Susan is always **on the go**. She has a family of seven to take care of. 蘇珊總是忙個不停，她有一家七口需要照顧。

come out of one's shell 變得對身邊的人和事感興趣，不再羞怯

- I am glad that my brother has **come out of his shell** after becoming a scout. 我很高興弟弟成為童軍後不再羞怯。

開（電器） open vs turn on

中式英語大透視

中文的「開 / 關」常與英文的 **open / close** 對應，如：「打開雪櫃」是 **open the fridge**；關門是 **close the door**。但是，不是所有情況兩種語言也對應，尤其在開關電器時，如：「開 / 關電視」不是 **open / close the TV**，而是 **turn on / off the TV**。其他同義詞包括 **switch on / off**、**power on / off**。另外，**turn off** 亦可寫成 **shut down**。

地道英文這樣說

turn on / off

• It is dangerous that you **turn on** the stove without opening the windows.
在不打開窗戶的情況下開爐灶是很危險的。

switch on / off

• Remember to **switch off** all lights before leaving home.
出門前記得關掉所有燈。

power on / off

• Which button should I press to **power on** this vacuum cleaner?
我該按下哪個按鈕來開啟吸塵機？

shut down

• You can try **shutting down** the computer when it freezes.
電腦當機時，可嘗試關閉電源。

增潤詞彙加分站

在英文世界，有一些有趣的片語與 **on** 和 **off** 有關，例如：

on and off 斷斷續續

• Sara works as a salesperson **on and off**. She spends most of her time painting.
莎莉斷斷續續地當售貨員。她大部分時間都花在畫畫上。

帶走（某物） take vs bring

我們經常混淆 take 和 bring 這兩個動詞。Take 指「帶走；拿走」，即由一處拿走某物到另一處。Bring 指「帶來；拿來」，即由一處拿來某物。舉例說，**Remember to take the umbrella with you.** 的 **take** 指帶走雨傘；而 **Please bring the spare keys to me.** 的 **bring** 指帶上備用鑰匙到某處。

地道英文這樣說

take

- I have found a purse on the street. I am taking it to the police station.
  我在街上拾到一個錢包。我正在拿它到警察局。

bring

- Mum, can you bring me the violin? I forgot to take it with me this morning.
  媽媽，你能把小提琴拿給我嗎？今早我忘記帶上它。

增潤詞彙加分站

另一組常被混淆的字是 hold 和 carry。Hold 指將某物拿在手中或懷裏，通常停留在某處；而 carry 指用手握住或背着某人或物，並把某人或物運送到另一個地方。

hold

- Can you hold my books and wait for me here?
  你能拿我的書在這裏等我嗎？

carry

- We carried heavy sand bags and went up the hill for our training yesterday.
  昨天我們背着沉重的沙袋上山訓練。

快速地 fastly vs fast

中文的副詞常以「地」作尾，如：美麗地、勤快地、積極地。而英文也有類似情況，我們可以在形容詞 (adjectives) 末尾加上 ly 來構成副詞 (adverbs)，如：beautifully、diligently、actively。但是，有一些副詞是例外，如 fast、hard 和 high，它們既是形容詞，亦是副詞，我們要多加留意，不能以偏概全。

地道英文這樣說

fast 很快地；快的

- [副詞] Sarah ran **fast** on the school Sports Day.
  莎拉在學校運動會上跑得很快。

- [形容詞] Sarah is a very **fast** runner.
  莎拉是一位非常快的跑手。

hard 努力地；艱苦的

- [副詞] I studied **hard** for the Maths exam, but I could barely get a pass.
  我為數學考試努力溫習，但只勉強及格。

- [形容詞] It takes lots of **hard** work to finish the renovation.
  完成翻新工程需要付出大量辛勤的工夫。

high 很高地；高的

- [副詞] I can jump pretty **high**.
  我可以跳得很高。

- [形容詞] Yet, the fence is too **high** for me to jump over.
  但是，柵欄太高了，我跳不過去。

增潤詞彙加分站

雖然 hard 和 high 可作副詞用，但是 hardly 和 highly 也真實存在，同樣是副詞，不過意思跟原本的形容詞不同。Hardly 解作「幾乎不能；僅僅」；highly 指「非常；很大程度上；很高水平上」。

友善地

friendly vs friendlily

Friend 是名詞，指「朋友」；friendly 是形容詞，指「友善的」；friendlily 則是副詞，指「友善地」。由於 friendly 後面有 ly，人們常誤以為它是副詞，但其實它是形容詞，就如 silly 和 ugly。如要寫成副詞，我們需把 y 變成 i，再後接 ly，即 friendlily、sillily 和 uglily。

地道英文這樣說

friend 朋友；friendly 友善的；friendlily 友善地

- Karen has been **friends** with me since we were little. Her parents are very **friendly**.
  凱倫從小就是我的朋友，她的父母非常友善。

- Cara looked at the puppy **friendlily** and lovingly.
  卡拉友善慈愛地看着小狗。

silly 愚蠢的；sillily 愚蠢地

- Don't be **silly**. You won't lose weight if you don't do exercise.
  別傻了，不做運動是無法減重的。

- Tom talks **sillily** whenever he gets drunk.
  湯姆一喝醉就說傻話。

ugly 醜陋的；uglily 醜陋地

- The **ugly** duckling later became a beautiful swan.
  醜小鴨後來變成了美麗的天鵝。

- The man **uglily** lied to his wife and took all her money away.
  那男子醜陋地對妻子說謊，並拿走了她所有金錢。

增潤詞彙加分站

由於 friendlily、sillily 和 uglily 發音困難，實際上不常使用。我們通常會稍微修改字詞，用 in a / an + adj. + manner 來表達相同意思。例如：friendlily 會改寫成 in a friendly manner。

eat medicine vs take medicine

不論是中文還是英文，動詞和名詞的搭配往往有既定組合，切忌把中文慣用的字詞搭配直接套進英文。例如，「吃藥」不是 eat medicine，而是 take medicine；「預約」不是 take an appointment，而是 make an appointment。

地道英文這樣說

take medicine

- We should take medicine according to the dosage and frequency suggested by our doctors.
  我們應依照醫生建議的劑量和次數服藥。

make an appointment

- I have made an appointment with Dr. Watson.
  我已與華生醫生預約好了。

增潤詞彙加分站

Do 可說是英文裏的「百搭動詞」，能搭配很多不同的名詞，例如：

do the dishes 洗碗

- Who is going to do the dishes this evening?
  今天晚上誰來洗碗？

do some reading 閱讀

- Hannah does some reading before bedtime every night.
  漢娜每晚睡覺前都會閱讀。

do some writing 寫作

- Mike does some writing and posts his stories online every weekend. 麥克每個周末都會寫作，並將故事發布到網上。

do harm 傷害

- Be honest to your mum. It won't do you any harm.
  對媽媽誠實吧，這不會對你造成任何傷害。

聽到噪音 listen to noises vs hear noises

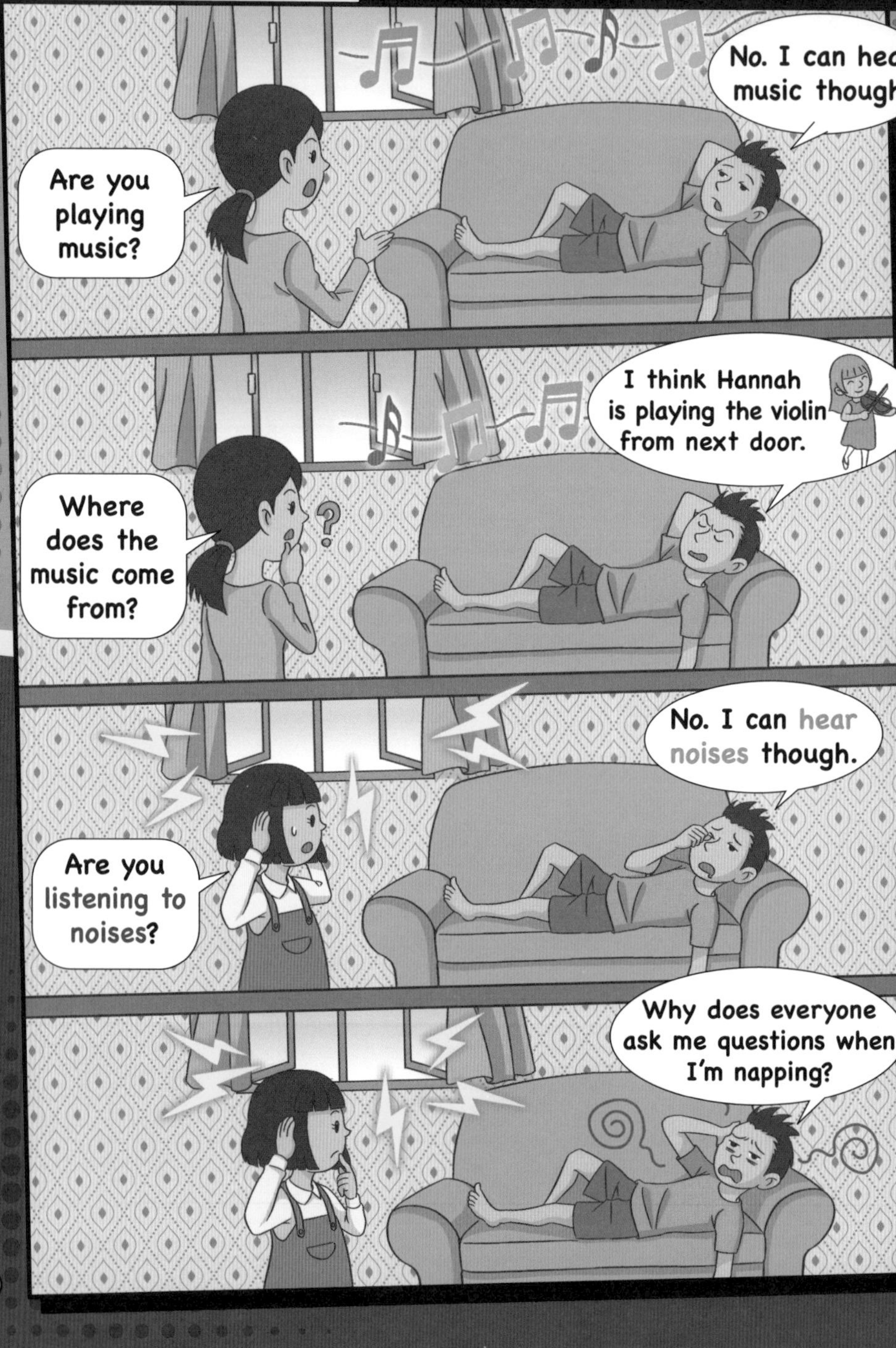

中文的「聽」包括了「聆聽」和「聽到」的意思，而英文沒有一個字可同時涵蓋這兩個意思。表達專注聆聽或集中在某種聲音時，我們通常會用 listen，後接介詞 to。表達聲音傳進耳朵，但不是我們想要聽到時，則用 hear。

在漫畫中，音樂和噪音都不是男孩想聽到的，所以用 hear。在一般情況下，noises 多搭配 hear，因為沒有人會主動聆聽噪音；music 多搭配 listen，因為多數是我們主動播放音樂。説到底，我們需按實際情景選擇動詞，不能一概而論。

地道英文這樣說

hear

• I **heard** somebody scream from next door. Should I call the police? 我聽到隔壁有人尖叫，我該報警嗎？

listen

• Grandpa likes **listening** to the radio every morning.
爺爺喜歡每天早上聽收音機廣播。

增潤詞彙加分站

有些英文動詞翻譯成中文時，意思一樣，但用法不同，如下：

talk 說話（通常兩個人或以上，雙方互相交流發言）

• Darren and Sara are **talking** about the new game they played last night. 達倫和薩拉正在談論他們昨晚玩的新遊戲。

speak 說話（着重說話一方，用於較為正式的場合）

• Principal Leung **spoke** about organising a game day after the exam weeks in the morning assembly.
梁校長在早會談到在考試周後舉辦遊戲日。

What are you busying doing?

We are making a project.

We are working on a project, not making a project.

Do you need to make a survey?

Yes, we are doing a survey, but not making a survey.

Mum, can you take part in our survey? Please fill out this for us.

我們時常説「做 project / 專題研習」，譯成英文時，很自然以 make 來搭配 project，但這並不正確，地道的字詞搭配應該是 do / work on a project。類似情況出現在「做問卷調查」，我們不能説 make a survey，而要説 do / conduct / carry out a survey。這些字詞搭配約定俗成，我們要多接觸地道英語，一點一滴累積語感，才能避免犯錯。

地道英文這樣說

do / work on a project

• Hayden was busy **working on a project**. Don't disturb him.
海頓正忙於做專題研習，不要打擾他。

do / conduct / carry out a survey

• Dr. Lee is **conducting a survey** on diet. He targets to have 500 participants. 李博士正在進行飲食調查，目標有 500 人參與。

增潤詞彙加分站

完成專題研習牽涉不同步驟和過程，以下是相關的字詞搭配。

collect data 收集資料

• Jeffrey and I tried **collecting data** through a survey and interviews. 卓飛和我嘗試透過調查和訪問來收集資料。

give advice 給予建議

• Can you **give** me some **advice** on how to write a report?
你能給我一些寫報告的建議嗎？

give a presentation 發表演講

• My group is going to **give a presentation** next week that will conclude our project.
我的小組將於下周發表演講，總結我們的專題研習。

> I bought this handbag online at a very expensive price. Isn't it nice?

> Cindy, your handbag was bought at a cheap price, right?

> Mine cost me about $1000, not a low price to me.

> An online shop sold fake luxury handbags at very high prices...

> I've bought a fake handbag.

「高」和「低」在不同的情況下，需用不同的英文字來表達。形容價格高或低時，我們會用 high price 或 low price，而不是 expensive price 或 cheap price。又例如，談論生產成本時，會用 high cost 和 low cost。而 expensive 和 cheap 是用來形容產品，如 expensive handbag 和 cheap earrings。

地道英文這樣說

high price; low price

• The price of this car is so high that I can't afford it.
這輛車的價格太高昂了，我買不起。

• Clara went to Milan and bought this designer's purse at a low price. 卡娜去米蘭以低價買了這個名師設計的錢包。

high cost; low cost

• It is really high cost to run a physical store.
經營實體店舖的成本確實很高。

• You can learn how to play the piano at a low cost through apps. 你可透過手機應用程式以低成本學習彈鋼琴。

expensive; cheap

• How much is this dress? It looks expensive.
這條連身裙多少錢？它看起來很昂貴。

• I bought this T-shirt at ten dollars, but it doesn't look cheap.
我用了十元買這件 T 恤，但它看上去一點也不像便宜貨。

增潤詞彙加分站

諺語 high and low 指「到處」，通常前面加動詞 hunt 或 search。

• Mum has been searching high and low for her lost earrings.
媽媽一直到處尋找她不見了的耳環。

高山

tall mountain vs high mountain

That's a high mountain. We will arrive there in two hours.

Dad, that's a very tall mountain.

Mum, let's sit under the high tree. I want to eat a sandwich.

That's a tall tree, my dear.

You are a tall boy now.

We were here four years ago. You were about this tall.

「高」除了形容價格，也可以形容人和物的高度，如「高個子的男孩」和「高山」；在英語，我們主要會用 high 和 tall。**High** 可用來形容山，如 high mountain，以及離地較高的物件，如 high wall、high fence、high ceiling 等。而 **tall** 則用來形容人，如 tall girl，以及外形高瘦的物件，如 tall tree 和 tall building。

地道英文這樣說

high

- Victoria Peak is one of the **high hills** in Hong Kong.
  太平山是香港的高山之一。

- The thieves entered the estate by climbing over the **high walls**.
  竊賊翻過高牆進入莊園。

tall

- What is the name of the **tall girl** in pink?
  那個穿粉紅色衣服的高個子女孩叫什麼名字？

- These **tall trees** are about 200 years old.
  這些高大的樹木已有大約 200 年的樹齡。

增潤詞彙加分站

Tall 亦有一些特別的意思，我們來看看以下慣用語。

tall order 艱巨的任務

- It is a **tall order** for me to finish the essay in 24 hours.
  在 24 小時內完成這篇論文，對我來說是艱巨的任務。

tall story 難以置信的故事

- Grandpa likes telling us **tall stories** of his old days when he worked as a police officer.
  爺爺喜歡跟我們說他以前當警察時遇到的難以置信的事跡。

The coffee tastes horrible. It isn't thick enough! It's thin and tasteless.

Coffee can be strong, but not thick; It can also be weak, but not thin.

形容咖啡和茶的濃淡程度時，我們或會誤用 **thick** 和 **thin**。其實，應該用 **strong** 來形容咖啡茶味道濃烈，用 weak 來形容淡而無味。不過，形容湯的質感時，就可用 **thick** 和 **thin**。**Thick soup** 指濃湯，即多材料的湯，而 **thin soup** 指清湯，即已被隔走材料的湯。由此可見，**thick** 和 **thin** 可描述飲料的質感，但不能形容其味道。

地道英文這樣說

strong coffee / tea; weak coffee / tea

- This **tea** is **strong**. It keeps me from dozing off at work.
  這杯茶很濃，讓我工作時不會打瞌睡。

- My **coffee** tastes so **weak**. They should have added more coffee grinds. 我的咖啡味道很淡，他們應該添加多些咖啡粉。

thick soup; thin soup

- Clam Chowder is my favourite **thick soup**. It's creamy with lots of ingredients. 周打蜆湯是我最喜歡的濃湯，口感綿滑，材料豐富。

- Chicken broth is a very useful **thin soup**. Mum always uses it to make different kinds of dishes.
  雞湯是非常有用的清湯，媽媽常用它做不同菜餚。

增潤詞彙加分站

在英語世界，有很多字詞可形容咖啡和茶的味道，例如：

rich in flavour 味道濃郁

- This latte is so **rich in flavour**. I am addicted to it.
  這杯拿鐵咖啡的味道很濃郁，我喝上癮了。

earthy 有大自然的味道

- I love oolong tea because it tastes **earthy** and refreshing.
  我喜歡烏龍茶，因為味道樸實清爽。

My name is Kevin. Nice to meet you.

I'm Leo. Nice to meet you too.

My class is big. There are 35 students in my class.

My class is big too. My class has 36 students.

What do you mean?

Oh! I mean that there are 36 students in my class.

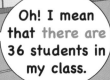

Have 和 has 多用來表達我們擁有的東西，或身體和物件的特徵，但我們時常以偏概全，把「有」誤譯作 have 或 has，如「我班有 30 名學生。」譯成 My class has 30 students. 在英語，我們應運用 There is / are ... 這句式，説成 There are 30 students in my class.

地道英文這樣説

I / We / They / You have

- I have a beautiful voice. 我有一把美麗的聲音。

- We have a cat. 我們有一隻貓。

He / She / It has

- Beware of that giant dog. It has very sharp teeth.
  小心那隻大狗，牠有非常鋒利的牙齒。

- Susan is the oldest child at home. She has two younger brothers. 蘇珊是家裏最大的孩子，她有兩個弟弟。

There is / There are ...

- There is a beautiful flower between these two rocks.
  這兩塊石頭之間有一朵美麗的花朵。

- There are five members in my family. 我家有五口人。

增潤詞彙加分站

Have 時常出現在英文慣用語，看看以下例子：

have a heart of gold 擁有慈悲的心

- My mum has a heart of gold. She is always generous and forgiving. 我媽媽擁有慈悲的心，總是慷慨寬容。

我沒事。

No, I am OK. vs Yes, I am OK.

Are you OK?

No, I am OK.

But you said "no".

I mean "No worries. I am OK."

Next time, you should say "Yes, I am OK." or "No, I am not OK."

OK.

在中文日常對話，我們問別人「你還好嗎？」，別人通常回答「沒事，我還好。」因為慣於這樣回答，當外國人問我們 **Are you OK?** 我們很自然回答 No, I am OK. 然而，**No** 一定要配 **not**，即是 No, I am not OK. 如沒事，則回答 Yes, I am OK. 同樣情況也可能發生在其他的一般疑問句 (Yes-no questions)，因此要聽清楚問題才回答。

地道英文這樣說

Yes, I am OK. / No, I am not OK.

- "You look upset. Are you OK?" David asked Sally.
  "**No, I am not OK.** I failed my English exam," answered Sally.
  大衞問莎莉：「你看起來很沮喪。你還好嗎？」
  莎莉回答：「不，我不好。我英文考試不及格。」

Yes, I do. / No, I do not.

- "Did you forget to turn off the lights?" Mum asked me.
  "**Yes, I did.** Sorry about that," I replied.
  媽媽問我：「你忘記了關燈嗎？」
  我回答：「是的，我忘記了，對不起。」

增潤詞彙加分站

雖然一般疑問句的答案通常是 Yes 或 No，但是我們亦可以回答 Yes and no. 來表示「説不準；也是也不是」。

- "Did you enjoy the concert yesterday?" Yuki asked me.
  "**Yes and no.** I was thrilled to attend the live concert, but I sat too far away from the stage," I answered.
  由紀問我：「昨天的音樂會你喜歡嗎？」
  我回答說：「是喜歡的，但也有不喜歡的地方。我很高興能參與現場音樂會，但我的座位離舞台太遠了。」

Because I missed the bus, so I arrived school late. Please let me sit down.

Don't use "because" and "so" togther.

Although my English isn't good, but I will study hard. Please let me go to the classroom.

Don't use "although" and "but" together.

Although you don't like English, you still have to study hard. Read this.

中式英語大透視

「雖然……，但是……」和「因為……，所以……」是常見的中文句式，英文也有類似的句式。要特別注意的是，在同一句英文句子中，although（雖然）和 but（但是）不會同時出現。同樣，because（因為）和 so（所以）也不會同時出現。

地道英文這樣說

although; but

- **Although** the weather was bad, we enjoyed the picnic very much. 儘管天氣不好，我們還是非常享受野餐。

- The weather was bad, **but** we enjoyed the picnic very much. 天氣不好，但是我們非常享受野餐。

because; so

- Susan was over the moon **because** her dad bought her a new computer. 蘇珊欣喜若狂，因為爸爸買了一部新電腦給她。

- Susan's dad bought her a new computer, **so** she was over the moon. 爸爸買了一部新電腦給蘇珊，所以蘇珊欣喜若狂。

增潤詞彙加分站

英語有許多連接詞，看看以下例子，學習如何正確使用它們吧。

since 因為（用於句子開首和中間均可）

- **Since** Nathan wasn't tall enough to reach the cupboard, he asked his older brother for help.
由於內森不夠高，觸不到櫃子，所以他請哥哥幫忙。

however 不過（用於句子開首和中間均可）

- Peter injured his arm, **however**, he insisted to take the violin exam. 彼得的手受傷了，不過他堅持參加小提琴考試。

I yesterday ... vs I ... yesterday.

What did you do yesterday?

I yesterday played video games.

So, do you mean "you played video games yesterday"?

Yes.

What are you going to do after work today?

I today will play video games after work.

So, do you mean "you will play video games after work today"?

Yes, but I'd better get a coffee first.

我們有時將「今天」、「明天」、「昨天」放在主詞後面，即「我今天……」、「爸爸明天……」、「她昨天……」。譯成英文時，或會錯誤寫成 I today ...、Dad tomorrow ... 和 She yesterday ... 但是這些字詞通常放在句末或句首，不會放在主詞後面。

地道英文這樣說

yesterday

- Max and Mike explored the haunted house **yesterday**.
  麥克斯和麥克昨天去探險鬼屋。

- **Yesterday** I broke my mobile phone. 昨天我把手機弄壞了。

today

- It was a rainy day **today**. 今天是下雨天。

- **Today** I went to the zoo. 今天我去了動物園。

tomorrow

- Are you going to join us for movie **tomorrow**?
  你明天要跟我們一起看電影嗎？

- **Tomorrow** my mum is going to meet with my class teacher.
  明天我媽媽要去見班主任。

增潤詞彙加分站

Yesterday、today 和 tomorrow 本身也可以是主詞，見以下諺語。

Yesterday isn't soon enough. 事情需要儘快處理

- The bills were due yesterday. **Yesterday isn't soon enough.**
  賬單昨天到期了，必須儘快付清。

One today is worth two tomorrows. 把握今天勝過兩個明天

- **One today is worth two tomorrows**, so seize the day.
  把握今天勝過兩個明天，所以抓住當下吧。

今天下雨。

Today is rainy. vs It is rainy today.

How was your day, my dear?

Today was a bad day.

Do you mean "you had a bad day today"?

Yes. We couldn't play in the playground.

Plus, because today is rainy.

It is rainy today, but rainy days can be fun too!

我們談論天氣時，習慣用「今天」作為主語，例如「今天下雨」。
然而，用英語時，主語應該使用 it，並將 today 放在句末，例如
It is a rainy day today. / It is rainy today.

地道英文這樣說

today

- It was very foggy **today**. It was dangerous to drive in such weather. 今天很大霧，在這樣的天氣駕駛很危險。

- Michelle had a tiring day **today**. She had worked over 12 hours. 米歇爾今天辛苦了一天，她已經工作了 12 個小時以上。

tomorrow

- It will be rainy **tomorrow**, so remember to take an umbrella with you. 明天下雨，記得帶傘。

- It will be so fun **tomorrow** because we are going cycling. 明天會很有趣，因為我們要去騎單車。

yesterday

- Andy had a frustrating day **yesterday**. He lost his mobile phone and he failed his test.
  安迪昨天很沮喪。他丟了手機，而且測驗不及格。

- It was stormy and rainy **yesterday**. We spent the day watching TV at home. 昨天颳暴風雨。我們整天在家看電視。

增潤詞彙加分站

英語中有很多與「天氣」有關的諺語，例如：

under the weather 感到不適

- He is feeling **under the weather**. He is not going to school today. 他感到不適，今天不去上學了。

What animal do you like?

I am like cats.

Jason, "I am like cats" means "you look like a cat".

What animal does your mother like?

My mum likes cats. She is like a cat too.

When she is not angry, she is like a cat. Yet, when she is angry, she is like a tigress!

在中文，「我喜歡貓」和「我像貓」有明顯的差異。然而，在英語，**like** 同時出現在 I like cats. 和 I am like a cat. 令我們容易混淆這兩句句子的意思。在前一句，**like** 是動詞，意思是「喜歡」；在後一句，**am** 是動詞，**like** 是介詞，解作「像」。

地道英文這樣說

like 喜歡 [動詞]

- Mike **likes** children, so he wants to be a teacher when he grows up. 麥克喜歡孩子，所以他長大後想當老師。

- We **like** listening to the stories told by Mr. Yeung. 我們都喜歡聽楊老師講故事。

like 像 [介詞]

- Kelly sings **like** an angel. She has a stunning voice. 凱莉的歌聲就像天使，擁有天籟之音。

- My brother looks **like** my dad, but I look completely different from them. 哥哥長得像爸爸，但我跟他們長得完全不一樣。

增潤詞彙加分站

英語還有許多單字或短語可用來表達「喜歡」和「像」。

be fond of 喜歡

- Benny **is** very **fond of** ball games. He played football well. 班尼熱愛球類運動，擅長踢足球。

be keen on 熱衷於

- Tom **is keen on** collecting stamps from around the world. 湯姆熱衷於收集世界各地的郵票。

similar to 像

- Your school bag looks **similar to** mine, but mine has a red strip at the top. 你的書包和我的很像，但我的書包頂端有一條紅色帶。

趣味漫畫學英語
中式英語全破解
Chinglish

作　　者：Agnes Chan
插　　圖：岑卓華
責任編輯：黃稔茵
美術設計：劉麗萍
出　　版：新雅文化事業有限公司
　　　　　香港英皇道 499 號北角工業大廈 18 樓
　　　　　電話：(852) 2138 7998
　　　　　傳真：(852) 2597 4003
　　　　　網址：http://www.sunya.com.hk
　　　　　電郵：marketing@sunya.com.hk
發　　行：香港聯合書刊物流有限公司
　　　　　香港荃灣德士古道 220-248 號荃灣工業中心 16 樓
　　　　　電話：(852) 2150 2100
　　　　　傳真：(852) 2407 3062
　　　　　電郵：info@suplogistics.com.hk
印　　刷：中華商務彩色印刷有限公司
　　　　　香港新界大埔汀麗路 36 號
版　　次：二〇二四年六月初版

ISBN: 978-962-08-8390-3
18/F, North Point Industrial Building, 499 King's Road, Hong Kong
Published in Hong Kong SAR, China
Printed in China